COWBOYS

COWBOYS

by Elaine Landau

FRANKLIN WATTS
NEW YORK | LONDON | TORONTO | SYDNEY
A FIRST BOOK | 1990

Cover photograph courtesy of: Bettmann Archive

Photographs courtesy of: Photo Researchers:
pp. 10 (Dean Krakel), 13 (Pat & Tom Leeson),
20 (Guy Gillette), 34 & 35 (Earl Scott), 38
(R. Rowan); Historical Picture Service: pp. 2, 3, 14,
15, 46; New York Public Library Picture Collection:
pp. 17, 24, 26, 27, 29, 32, 51, 54, 55;
Bettmann Archive: pp. 18, 19, 41, 43; The Kansas State
Historical Society: pp. 37, 45, 48, 50.

Library of Congress Cataloging-in-Publication Data

Landau, Elaine.
Cowboys / by Elaine Landau.
p.   cm. — (A First book)
Includes bibliographical references.
Summary: Depicts how cowboys lived in the Old West, describes
their methods of raising cattle, and discusses their pastimes.
ISBN 0-531-10866-X
1. Cowboys—West (U.S.)—Juvenile literature.   2. Frontier and
pioneer life—West (U.S.)—Juvenile literature.   3. West (U.S.)—Social life and customs—Juvenile literature.   [1. Cowboys.
2. Frontier and pioneer life—West (U.S.)   3. West (U.S.)—Social
life and customs.]   1. Title.   II. Series.
F596.L358   1990
978—dc20   90-31025 CIPAC

Also by Elaine Landau

Alzheimer's Disease

Black Market Adoption
and the Sale of Children

Lyme Disease

Nazi War Criminals

The Sioux

Surrogate Mothers

Tropical Rain Forests
Around the World

We Have AIDS

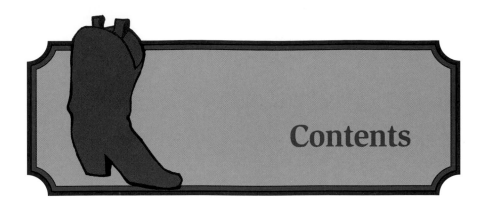

Contents

Chapter One
Cowboys of the American West 11

Chapter Two
Home on the Range 23

Chapter Three
The Roundup 31

Chapter Four
The Trail Drive 40

Chapter Five
The End of a Golden Age 53

Glossary 58

For Further Reading 60

Index 61

COWBOYS

At sunrise, this mounted cowboy is
ready to begin his long day's work.
In the early West, cowboys were often
expected to work from sunup to sunset

1 Cowboys of the American West

AT A ROUNDUP, the average workday began just before dawn. There, in the darkness, the cook would light a lantern and begin to heat the five-gallon coffeepot over a shallow ditch built for a cooking fire.

The men who worked on the range knew better than to fault another man's cooking, but they did expect their meals to be ready on time. Knowing this, a Western roundup cook worked quickly. He'd prepare the beans, bacon, and biscuits to be placed in a hot oven.

Meanwhile, the camp began to buzz with activity. The men rose from their bedrolls on the ground and pulled on their pants and boots.

Some men used basins to wash themselves in the morning. Others just drew a cup of water from the cook's barrel and splashed it on their faces. The men passed a towel around for everyone to use. There might be a comb available for those who didn't have their own.

These early cowboys of the American West were usually young men. Some were barely out of their teens. But youth seems to be the only thing many cowboys had in common, because in other ways they were a varied group. Some were former Confederate and Union soldiers who had headed West after the Civil War. Many cowboys were members of minority groups, including immigrants from Europe and Asia. There were outstanding Indian, Mexican, and black cowboys. In fact, over a third of the cowboys in the early West were either black or Mexican. Many of the black cowboys had once been slaves.

For a twenty-year period, from the mid-1860s to the mid-1880s, cowboys were crucial to the growth of the West's cattle business. Ranchers depended on cowboys to tend their cattle on the open range. The open range was a vast area of unfenced land that contained only a handful of communities. It extended across the Great Plains

As in the early West, here modern Montana
cowboys tend their ranch's cattle. The
bright yellow flowers are called mule's
ears. The cattle graze on
the grass and flowers.

of North America from Mexico to Canada and from Kansas to the Rockies.

The grasslands of the open range seemed endless, and were covered with cattle. Ranchers turned their herds out on the open range, where

This painting entitled Cattle Raising on Our Great Plains *shows cowboys tending cattle on the open range in Texas.*

the animals fattened themselves by grazing. Cattle had to be fattened before being sold.

Another of the cowboys' important duties was the trail drives. During a trail drive, cowboys would move thousands of cattle across the range to railroad stations. From there, the cattle were shipped to markets for sale in the East.

A cowboy's work could be difficult and dangerous. There were hardships involved in tending cattle on the open range. Very often the animals got into serious trouble, and it was up to the cowboys to rescue them.

Sometimes the cowboys had to pull cattle from quicksand or drag them from mud ditches after heavy rainstorms. The men cared for sick and injured cattle, often doing much of what *veterinarians* do today to make animals well.

It was not unusual for a cowboy to be hurt during a day's work, and sometimes the injuries were serious or even crippling. Many cowboys suffered broken bones after being kicked or thrown by a spirited horse. There were roping accidents as well. At times, cowboys were

As shown in this painting, some horses were especially difficult to tame. A "high roller" was a spirited horse who would buck or leap high into the air to throw the cowboy who mounted it.

Before a horse could be ridden,
it had to be tamed, or "broken."
Wild horses would leap or kick
to throw a rider off its back.
Cowboys who tamed wild horses
were called broncobusters.

hurt or killed while working with cattle, and some were trampled to death by stampeding herds.

Sick or injured cowboys rarely had a chance to see a doctor. The few doctors in the West usually worked in distant towns, so cowboys had to learn to treat themselves. Some managed well on their own. Others suffered because they lacked essential medical knowledge. All types of wounds and broken bones were common on the open range. If a wound wasn't properly cleaned and wrapped, infection could easily set in. A cowboy with a broken leg could only hope that it would heal properly. If the bone wasn't cor-

Some of the clothing shown here was also worn by cowboys of the early West. Cowboys preferred jackets to coats because they were less bulky. Vests with pockets helped the cowboys carry small, useful items. Their bandannas or neckerchiefs shielded them from the sun as they worked outdoors for long hours.

rectly set, the injured cowboy might be left with a permanent limp.

There are many books and Hollywood movies about the cowboy's dashing and exciting adventures. These stories are usually not based on facts. Actually, cowboys spent much of their time away from other people. These overworked and underpaid men were often bored and lonely. On a trail drive to the railroad station, the cowboy might be isolated from civilization for over three months at a time. While working on the range, it was not uncommon for a cowboy to go long periods without seeing anyone but the handful of men he worked with. The vast majority of ranches were many miles away from even the tiniest town or outpost.

2

Home on the Range

COWBOYS PUT IN LONG HOURS to earn their pay. Caring for the ranch owner's cattle meant that the cowboy had to know how to perform many different tasks. Among these were dehorning animals as well as protecting them from wolves.

Cattle roamed and grazed freely on the open range. The animals might wander long distances in various directions. It was the cowboy's responsibility to bring them back.

To do this, ranch owners had a number of small outposts set up at various points bordering their land. These stations were known as line camps. The cowboys assigned to work the various camps were called line riders. Their duties included patrolling a special area. These cow-

boys combed the territory for sick cows and calves. It was also their job to be on the lookout for cattle thieves. Ranchers could not afford to lose their animals to these *rustlers,* who would steal cattle and later sell them for profit.

Throughout the summer months, cowboys were alert to the risk of fire on the open range. During long spells of extremely hot weather, the land became dry and scorched. Without warning, fires broke out and quickly spread, often destroying grass and cattle over large areas. Cowboys had to fight these fires and try to save the cattle. In the summer, cowboys also had to inspect the cattle's *water holes* in case some had dried up.

Besides caring for cattle, cowboys did other work around the ranch. This was especially true in the winter when things slowed down. Ranch owners dismissed unneeded help. The remain-

The cowboy's rope, called a lariat, dangled from his saddle as he rode the range. He'd use his lariat to rope cattle as well as for other jobs.

In this oil painting called One in Every Bunch, a cowboy ropes a young cow who has just escaped from the pen shown in the background.

ing cowboys cut ice on the water holes. They also drove cattle onto snow-free grass and brought in sick cows and calves. Cowboys maintained ranch equipment and repaired bridles and harnesses.

Most cowboys were proud, independent, and loyal to the rancher they worked for. A cowboy took pride in how he performed on the range. He mastered special skills and did not consider himself a common laborer. A cowboy was willing to squelch prairie fires, halt thunderous stampedes, or stand guard over the cattle in sleet or rain—but he didn't want to feed the hogs!

While at the ranch, cowboys lived in a *bunkhouse* that offered few comforts. It was usually a poorly built structure without fancy trappings. During the winter months, the men might feel the biting cold down to their bones. It was hard to stop the freezing air from blowing in.

A bunkhouse had just one room, which wasn't very large. Many bunkhouses were dirty and sloppily kept. Cowboys had to share their living quarters with bedbugs and lice.

Commonly, cowboys didn't call one another by their real names. Within his first week at the bunkhouse, a new man was generally given a nickname. Often the name described something

Cowboys working at the ranch.
In the background is the bunkhouse
where they slept, the cookhouse
where they ate, and pens
in which horses and other
animals were sometimes kept.

about him. For example, a redhead might be called "Red" or "Sunset," and a sorrowful-looking man "Gloomy." Someone who talked a lot was usually given the nickname "Lippy" or "Wagon Tongue." Other common cowboy names were "Slim," "Baldy," "Shorty," "Wildcat," and "Pecos." Whether or not the cowboy liked the nickname the others picked for him, it usually stuck.

There wasn't much to do at a bunkhouse in the evenings. The cowboys tried to pass the time reading or gambling for small stakes among themselves. After a full day's work, though, the men were usually exhausted. Most went to bed early.

3 The Roundup

AMONG THE HIGHLIGHTS of the cowboy's life was the *roundup*. Roundups were held twice a year—in the spring and in the fall. At the spring roundup, new calves were branded. During the fall roundup, cattle were branded and selected for sale. Ranch owners formed special associations to determine the exact dates for the roundups.

Cattle from the various ranches grazed together on the range. During roundups, cowboys from different areas worked together to bring in the animals. Teams of cowboys rode off in different directions to look for cattle. Then all the animals were driven to one location.

Once the animals had been rounded up, the cowboys picked out the cattle belonging to their ranches. To separate the cattle from the different ranches, cowboys rode specially trained horses called "cutting horses." Usually only three or four men were used for this task. Too many "cutters" would frighten or panic the cattle.

As the cutters worked, the other cowboys circled the herd trying to keep the animals together. Since there weren't any holding pens on the range, the cattle separated into "cuts" had to be kept away from the others.

After the cattle had been sorted out by *brand,* the newborn calves were branded. The cowboys drove the young calves to a fire, where the branding irons had been heated. A cowboy placed

Rounding up cattle for the trail drives was exhausting work. Yet many cowboys looked forward to this break from their often solitary duties. As the men worked in teams, sometimes they would meet old friends who were now at different ranches.

At the Gamble Ranch in Nevada, modern-day cowboys round up cattle to be branded.

the hot iron to the calf's skin. This left the rancher's mark permanently on the animal. Each ranch had its own brand, which was registered with local officials. As further proof of owner-ship, all animals owned by a ranch were branded on the same body part, such as the left flank or the right side of the animal's jaw.

Branding the animals enabled the cowboys to identify and claim their ranch's cattle. It was important to know whom each cow belonged to, since before fencing became common, cows might stray for hundreds of miles. If an honest person found a stray near his property, he could check the cow's brand and return the animal to its rightful owner.

Branding also helped to prevent rustlers from stealing cattle. But sometimes rustlers tried to alter the stray cow's brand to make it look like their own. Stealing cattle was a serious offense, and those caught were often punished swiftly and severely. Sometimes powerful ranch owners hired gunmen to shoot rustlers caught in the act. In other instances, the rustlers were captured and hanged.

Even with branding, ranchers were bound to lose some of their cattle to rustlers, wild ani-mals, and accidents on the range. A rancher

Texas cowboys create a temporary corral for their horses. There weren't any sturdy pens or corrals on the open range and cowboys needed to keep the animals from straying.

As in the early West, cowboys today still enjoy singing after work. Some modern cowboys also write poetry about their work and lives, which they read aloud at present-day cowboy poetry festivals!

carefully counted the cows he sent out to graze. But he knew what really mattered was the number of cows his men would eventually round up and send to market.

After the sun set at a roundup, the cowboys ate and spent some time together. The men shared stories of fighting, bucking contests, and wild cattle chases. Cowboys were well known for their practical jokes and tall tales. A cowboy might bring an accordion, fiddle, or banjo to a roundup. Mouth organs (harmonicas) were especially common. After enjoying one another's company for a time, the tired cowboys stumbled off to their beds.

At a roundup, the men slept outside in bedrolls on the ground. However, they never had a full night's rest. They were called two at a time to stand guard watching the herd.

4

The Trail Drive

THE ROUNDUP and the trail drive were perhaps the most important tasks performed by the cowboy for the ranch owner. During a trail drive, a cowboy moved two or three thousand cattle to a railroad station to be shipped to markets in the East. A number of different paths for transporting cattle were used. Some were as long as fifteen hundred miles. They usually ended in a Kansas cow town where a railway to the East ran. Among the best known of these paths was the Chisholm Trail.

Before the trail drive began, several ranchers got together to hire a trail boss. The cowboys from different ranches collected their cattle and turned the animals over to the trail boss.

A cowboy at work on
a trail drive. During a trail drive,
a cowboy spent nearly all his working
hours on horseback.

The trail boss was responsible for the trail drive and the cattle's welfare.

A trail boss had to know how to avoid dangerous accidents while on the drive as well as keep the respect of his men. Trail bosses were paid nearly five times as much as other cowboys on the drive.

The trail boss hired between ten and twelve cowboys and a cook to take with him. Only the very best men were selected to go on the long drive. Moving cattle hundreds of miles through the wilderness required strength, skill, and experience. Usually the trail boss also hired a very young cowboy as a wrangler. The wrangler tended to the fifty or more horses taken along for the cowboys' use. Few cowboys could afford a horse of their own. Instead they rode the ranch's horses. Since a cowboy used more than one horse, he generally didn't have a favorite or pet horse.

The cook stocked the *chuck wagon* for the trail drive. Chuck wagons were used during both roundups and trail drives. A chuck wagon was a covered wagon large enough to carry supplies for the long trip. Among other items, it contained food, drinking water, pots, pans, and

A cowboy rests against his bedroll
near the chuck wagon as the evening
meal is prepared. All the plates,
cups, and cooking utensils were made
of metal so they could be carried
long distances along bumpy trails
without being damaged.

eating utensils. The cowboy's bedrolls were also kept in the chuck wagon when not in use.

On a trail drive, the cowboys rode with the herds, guiding the animals as they kept them moving along. Cattle traveled slowly, usually only ten to fifteen miles a day. The cowboys often sang songs as they rode. They also sang to the animals at night. Singing helped to pass the time, and the sound of the men's voices soothed the cattle.

Few trail drives went smoothly. At many points along the way, the animals might panic. If that happened while the cattle were crossing a river, they'd begin to swim around in circles. At times, the raging rivers pulled cattle, cowboys, and horses downstream.

Any loud sudden sound or even a crack of thunder could frighten the cattle into a stampede. To stop the stampeding herd from racing ahead, the cowboys would quickly try to head them off. The men would ride in front of the animals and fire their guns into the air. The cowboys would also wave their hats to turn the frightened cattle around. Unfortunately, many cowboys were badly hurt or killed during stampedes.

This picture shows the vastness of a trail drive over a wide stretch of land. Here cowboys transport nearly 1,300 head of cattle to a cow town.

Trail drives through Indian country faced still other problems. Indian tribes, who had been robbed of their lands by the white settlers, tried to fight back. The Indians were especially angered by the sight of the ranchers' cattle grazing where their own buffalo had once been. Sometimes the Indians raided the cowboys' chuck wagons. They also stampeded the cattle.

The Indians kept whatever strays they found. Some demanded to be paid to round up the scattered cattle for the cowboys. Often tribes were anxious to protect what little land they had left. They insisted that the trail drives remain on narrow paths bordering their territory.

The workday on a trail drive might last for nearly fifteen hours. During much of that time, the cowboys remained on their horses as the fiercely hot sun blazed down on them. To make matters worse, the men often had to work

Cowboys try to halt a stampeding herd. Men in front, back, and alongside the raging cattle snap their whips on the ground to turn the animals back.

*Cowboys on a trail drive stop along the way to bathe
in a stream. It may be months before they arrive at a cow
town where they'll have a bath in a tub of hot water.*

through a haze of dust kicked up by the moving herds of cattle.

Each day the drive usually stopped just before the sun went down. On trail drives, as on roundups, the men took turns watching the herds throughout the night. If the animals stampeded during the night, the cowboys would be forced to go after them in total darkness. The men would have only the sound of racing hooves to guide them.

The trail drive ended when the cowboys finally reached a *cow town*. Here the cattle were sold for shipment and loaded onto a train. When some of the animals resisted entering the railway boxcars, the cowboys used sticks to prod them along. That's why cowboys are sometimes called *cowpokes* or cowpunchers.

After months on the trail, most cowboys looked forward to spending some time in town. They'd sleep in a real bed with sheets, have a shave, a haircut, and some good food. At a cow town, they had a chance to buy clean clothes. A cowboy might also want to relax and enjoy himself at a local *saloon*.

The cowboys were paid at the end of a trail drive. The average cowboy earned between thirty-five and forty dollars a month, so each man had

ABOVE: This 1871 picture shows cowboys loading cattle into railroad boxcars at the trail drive's end. This was the cowboy's final job before he could go out and enjoy himself in the cow town.

RIGHT: Cow towns in the early West were often rough, lawless places. Many inexperienced cowboys, who were no match for professional gamblers and outlaws, headed home both broke and brokenhearted. Notice how young the cowboy in this picture is.

about a hundred dollars coming to him. There were lots of things to buy in the cow towns of the Old West. Liquor was plentiful for a price. It was said that cowboys worked hard on the trail and drank hard in town. Gambling casinos and dance-hall girls were anxious to part the cowboy from his pay. It was not uncommon for a cowboy to spend all his earnings in a few days.

Although in Western movies cowboys are often shown with a gun, actually most cowboys didn't wear one. Cowboys on trail drives found a gun useful to turn back a stampede or shoot a rattlesnake. But generally, cowboys working on horseback much of the day didn't like the additional heaviness and bulk of a weapon.

Nevertheless, most cowboys did wear a gun when they reached a cow town at the end of the trail drive. They carried the weapon hoping to look more manly and gain the respect of others. Things could get rough in a cow town. Brawls broke out. Some cowboys were shot and killed. But most just returned to their life at the ranch once their money ran out.

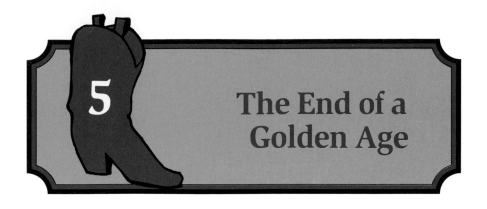

5

The End of a Golden Age

FOLLOWING THE CIVIL WAR, cowboys were extremely important to the West's growing cattle industry. However, in years to come, the cowboy's life greatly changed. At first, the grasslands had been plentiful, and most important, the winters had been mild. Cattle grazed and roamed on the range freely throughout the year.

But the winter of 1885–86 was brutally cold. Thousands of cattle froze to death. The harsh winter was followed by an unbearably hot and dry summer. Scores of animals starved to death as the springs dried up and grass became scant.

Next came the winter of 1886–87, which brought the worst snowstorms and blizzards the

This painting called The Fall of the Cowboy shows the freezing winter of 1886—87. The brutal season put many ranchers out of business and was an important factor in ending the golden age of the cowboy.

cowboys could remember. Tens of thousands of cattle starved and froze at temperatures of nearly fifty degrees below zero. In the spring, the cowboys found the rotting carcasses of the herds they'd tended. Ranchers no longer felt certain that their cattle would survive harsh winters on the plains.

Other changes were taking place as well. Once barbed wire came into use, the need for round-ups greatly lessened. Most ranchers no longer grazed their cattle on the open range. Instead, *barbed-wire* fences kept the animals in separate pastures. Fences also allowed large ranch owners to control vital water holes and streams.

As more settlers went West, people began to farm the land. The millions of free unclaimed acres the cattle had grazed on were now being carved up into homesteads. To stop the cattle herds from trampling their fields, farmers put up their own barbed-wire fences. At times, farmers even took up arms to fight the ranchers. Before long, the vast open range began to disappear.

Meanwhile, the railroad companies continued their expansion. They laid tracks across the country. Trail drives were no longer necessary to bring animals to shipping sites. It was soon possible to ship cattle directly from different areas. By the close of the 1880s, the Golden Age of America's Western cowboy was over.

Glossary

Barbed wire—a type of fencing that has sharp points

Brand—a marking burned on an animal with a hot iron to show ownership

Bunkhouse—the cowboys' sleeping quarters at the ranch

Chuck—food

Chuck wagon—a wagon taken on trail drives and roundups containing the cowboys' food, cooking equipment, bedrolls, and other necessary items

Cowpoke—another name for a cowboy. Cowboys were sometimes called cowpokes, or cowpunchers, because they used sticks to prod the cattle into railroad boxcars for shipment to the East.

Cow town—a Western town at the end of a trail drive from which cattle were shipped to the East by railway

Roundup—bringing cattle on the open range to a central place to be branded or taken on trail drives

Rustler—cattle thief

Saloon—a drinking establishment in the early West that usually provided liquor as well as gambling and entertainment

Veterinarian—a person professionally trained to medically treat and operate on animals

Water hole—a pool of water on the open range from which cattle or other animals drink

For Further Reading

Ames, Lee J. *Make Twenty-five Felt Tip Drawings Out West.* New York: Doubleday, 1980.

Fisher, Leonard E. *The Railroads.* New York: Holiday, 1979.

Martini, Terri. *Cowboys.* Chicago: Children's Press, 1981.

Moon, Dolly. *My Very First Book of Cowboy Songs.* Mineola, N.Y.: Dover, 1983.

Patent, Dorothy. *A Picture Book of Cows.* New York: Holiday, 1982.

Radlauer, Ed. *Cowboy Mania.* Chicago: Children's Press, 1981.

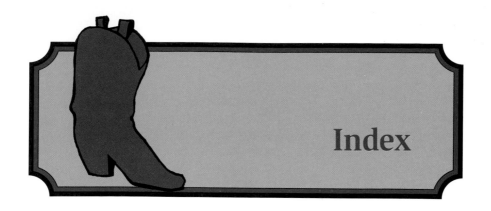

Index

Page numbers in *italics* refer to illustrations.

Barbed-wire fences, 56
Bathing in a stream, *48*
Black cowboys, 12
Branding cattle, 31, 33–36
Branding irons, 33
Bunkhouses, 28, *29*

Care of cattle, 16–22
Cattle thieves, 25, 36
Chisholm Trail, 40

Chuck wagons, *42*, 43, 44
Clothing worn by cowboys, *20*
Cooking, 11, 42
Cowpokes, 49
Cow towns, 49, *51*, 52
Cutting ice, 28
Cutting horses, 33

Dance-hall girls, 52
Drinking, 52

Fire fighting, 25

Gamble Ranch, Nevada, *34–35*
Gambling, 52
Golden Age of the Cowboy, 12, 57
Great Plains, 12–14
Guns, use of, 52

Horses, *17*, 18–19, 33, 42

Indian cowboys, 12
Indian tribes, hostility of, 47
Injuries to cowboys, 16–22, 44
Isolation, 22

Lariats, *24*
Line camps, 23
Line riding, 23–25

Medical care, 21–22
Mexican cowboys, 12
Montana cowboys, *13*
Music, 39, 44

Nicknames, 28–30

Open range, 12–14, 23, 56

Practical jokes, 39

Railroads, 16, 40, 49, 56
Ranch equipment, maintenance of, 28
Recreation, 30, 39, 44, 48–52
Roping cattle, *26–27*
Roundups, 11, 31, *32*, 33–39, 56

Settlers, 56
Shipping cattle to market, 16, 49, *50*, 56–57
Singing, 44
Stampedes, 44, *46*, 47, 49
Stories about cowboys, 22, 52

Texas cowboys, *14–15, 37*
Trail bosses, 40–43
Trail drives, 15–16, 22, 40, *41*, 43–44, *45*, 46–52, 56–57

Wages, 23, 49–52

Water holes, 25–28, 56
Weather hazards, 53, *54–55*, 56
Western movies, 22, 52
Wild animals, 23, 36
Workday, length of, *10*, 11, 23, 47–48
Wranglers, 43

About the Author

Elaine Landau received her B.A. degree in English and Journalism from New York University and a master's degree in Library and Information Science from Pratt Institute in New York City.

Ms. Landau has worked as a newspaper reporter, an editor, and a youth services librarian. She has written many books and articles for young people. Ms. Landau lives in Sparta, New Jersey.